WAY

Accelerated Reader

Book Level *1.6* AR Pts *0.5*

Lexile *300L*

DO NOT REMOVE
CARDS FROM POCKET

ABOUT THE BANK STREET READY-TO-READ SERIES

Seventy years of educational research and innovative teaching have given the Bank Street College of Education the reputation as America's most trusted name in early childhood education.

Because no two children are exactly alike in their development, we have designed the *Bank Street Ready-to-Read* series in three levels to accommodate the individual stages of reading readiness of children ages four through eight.

○ *Level 1:* GETTING READY TO READ—read-alouds for children who are taking their first steps toward reading.

● *Level 2:* READING TOGETHER—for children who are just beginning to read by themselves but may need a little help.

○ *Level 3:* I CAN READ IT MYSELF—for children who can read independently.

Our three levels make it easy to select the books most appropriate for a child's development and enable him or her to grow with the series step by step. The *Bank Street Ready-to-Read* books also overlap and reinforce each other, further encouraging the reading process.

We feel that making reading fun and enjoyable is the single most important thing that you can do to help children become good readers. And we hope you'll be a part of Bank Street's long tradition of learning through sharing.

The Bank Street College of Education

For Alexandra Rachel
—J.O.

THE SHOW-AND-TELL FROG
A Bantam Little Rooster Book / May 1992

Little Rooster is a trademark of Bantam Books,
a division of Bantam Doubleday Dell Publishing Group, Inc.

Series graphic design by Alex Jay / Studio J

Special thanks to James A. Levine and Betsy Gould.

Library of Congress Cataloging-in-Publication Data
Oppenheim, Joanne.
The show-and-tell-frog / by Joanne Oppenheim;
illustrated by Kate Duke.
p. cm. — (Bank Street Ready-to-Read)
"A Byron Preiss book,"
"A Bantam Little Rooster Book."
Summary: Allie finds a frog for show-and-tell, but he
disappears before she can take him to school.
ISBN 0-553-08134-9. — ISBN 0-553-35147-8 (pbk.)
[1. Frogs—Fiction. 2. Schools—Fiction.]
I. Duke, Kate, ill. II. Title. III. Series.
PZ7.0616Sh 1992
[E]—dc20
91-23680 CIP AC

Published simultaneously in the United States and Canada

PRINTED IN THE UNITED STATES OF AMERICA

0 9 8 7 6 5 4 3 2 1

Bank Street Ready-to-Read™

The
Show-and-Tell Frog

by Joanne Oppenheim
Illustrated by Kate Duke

A Byron Preiss Book

A BANTAM LITTLE ROOSTER BOOK
NEW YORK · TORONTO · LONDON · SYDNEY · AUCKLAND

On Sunday Allie found a green frog.
"Frog," she said, "you are going
to school with me.
You will be my show-and-tell frog!"

That night Allie put holes in a box
and put her frog inside.

She put the box under her bed.

But when Allie woke up
on Monday morning
the box was empty.
"My show-and-tell frog is gone!"
she cried.

Allie searched under her bed.

She looked behind the curtains

and inside her closet.

She could not find her frog
anywhere.

"Frog!" she said. "Where are you?"

"Allie!" her mom called.
"Where are you?"
"I'm right here," Allie called.
She did not want to tell her mom
that the frog was lost.

"Allie!" her mom called again.
"You will be late!"

"I'm coming," called Allie.
She grabbed her backpack.

Allie ran to the bus stop.
There was her friend Christopher.
He was carrying a big bag.
"What's in the bag?" Allie asked.

"Shells," said Christopher.
"I found them at the beach.
They are for show-and-tell.
Do you want to see them?"
"Sure," said Allie.

"Nice shells," Allie said.
"I found something, too.
But I lost it."

Just then the bus pulled up.
Christopher and Allie got on.

Allie sat next to her friend Jenny.
"Look what my grandpa made
for me," said Jenny.
"Wow," said Allie.
"That's a neat ring!
Can I try it on?"
"No," said Jenny.
"It's for show-and-tell.
I don't want to lose it."
Allie understood.
She wished she had not
lost her show-and-tell frog.

Allie got off the bus.
She bumped into her friend Annie.

"Watch it!" Annie yelled.
"You made me spill
my strawberries!
They are for show-and-tell!"
"I'll help pick them up,"
said Allie.
"This is a show-and-taste!"

Allie held the door for Annie.
The red strawberries
were a good show-and-tell.

But Allie wished she had
her show-and-tell frog.

Benjy had the first show-and-tell.
Allie liked the poster
Benjy got at the zoo.

She liked the pictures
Lisa showed of her baby brother.
Having a baby brother
would be fun,
Allie was thinking, when...

she felt something strange
brush against her leg.
"What's that?" yelled Jenny.

"Watch out!" screamed Annie.
"Help!" yelled Benjy.

"What's going on?"
asked the teacher.
"I've got it!" yelled Christopher.
"Get it out of here!" hollered Jenny.

"No! No! It's mine!"
shouted Allie.

Allie took her frog and
walked to the front of the class.
She said...

"This is my show-and-tell—
I mean,
my lost and found,
show-and-tell frog!"